Hi, Koo!

A Year of Seasons

Presented by Koo *and* Jon J Muth

Scholastic Press | New York

for Molly and Leo

Library of Congress Cataloging-in-Publication Data

Muth, Jon J

Hi, Koo!: A Year of Seasons / By Jon J Muth. — First edition.   pages cm

ISBN 978-0-545-16668-3 (hardcover)

1. Seasons — Juvenile poetry. 2. Haiku, American. 3. Children's poetry, American. I. Title.

PS3563.U849K66 2013   811'.54 — dc23   2012040378

10 9 8 7 6 5 4 3 2   14 15 16 17 18

Printed in Malaysia 108

First edition, March 2014

We gratefully acknowledge David Lanoue, President of The Haiku Society of America, for reviewing the Author's Note.

The display type was set in Neutra Display. The text was set in Monotype Bulmer.

Jon J Muth's artwork was created with watercolor and ink.

Book design by David Saylor

Author's Note

Haiku is a poetic form that originated in Japan. Traditionally it was made up of seventeen sound parts called *on* (pronounced OWN) — divided into three lines with five, then seven, then five *on*.

But English syllables and *on* are not the same. Haiku that are direct translations into English are often shorter than a total of seventeen syllables, unless a translator has chosen to create a five-seven-five pattern using English syllables.

Over time, haiku has evolved, so that many modern poets no longer adhere so rigidly to this structure. I have not restricted myself to the five-seven-five syllable pattern that many of us grew up learning haiku must be.

For me, haiku is like an instant captured in words — using sensory images. At its best, a haiku embodies a moment of emotion that reminds us that our own human nature is not separate from all of nature.

— JON J MUTH

P.S. If you look closely, you can find an alphabetical path
through the book by following the capitalized words in each haiku:
A — "Autumn," B — "Broom," C — "Coat," and so forth.

Fall

Autumn,
are you dreaming
of new clothes?

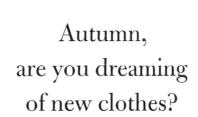

these leaves
fall forever
my Broom awaits

found!
in my Coat pocket a missing button
the wind's surprise

Dance through cold rain
then go home
to hot soup

Eating warm cookies
on a cold day
is easy

Friend, is that you
knocking at the door?
TWO!

snowfall
Gathers my footprints
I do a powdery stomp

snowball hits the stop sign
Heart beats faster
are we in trouble?

Icicles
reach down with dripping fingers
will they touch the ground?

in the snow
this cat vanishes
Just ears . . . and twitching tail

King!
my crown a gift
from a snowy branch

shadows getting Long
snowfall flutters around
the outside lamps

Morning crocuses!
winter is old now
and closes her doors

Spring

New leaves
new grass new sky
spring!

too much TV this winter
my eyes are square
let's go Out and play

flashlights
sparkle in Puddles
shadows climbing trees

Quiet and still
long enough
for birds to make nests?

Reading aloud
a favorite book
an audience of sparrows

killing a bug
afterward
feeling alone and Sad

Summer

Tiny lights
garden full of blinking stars
fireflies

summer morning
Up with the kite!
send the moon to bed!

Violet petal
caressing a cheek
butterfly kisses

Water catches
every thrown stone
skip-skip splash!

perilous tic-tac-toe
Xs and Os
sometimes become dragons

come again!
visit Your upside-down
fuzzy-eared friend

becoming so quiet
Zero sound
only breath